THE TALE OF
ELEAZAR

THE TALE OF
ELEAZAR

PRISCILLA NOBLE-MATHEWS

ARTIST NAME: SUSAN SHORTER

authorHOUSE®

AuthorHouse™
1663 Liberty Drive
Bloomington, IN 47403
www.authorhouse.com
Phone: 1-800-839-8640

Published by AuthorHouse   10/12/2012

ISBN: 978-1-4685-8227-7 (sc)
ISBN: 978-1-4685-8228-4 (e)

Artist name: Susan Shorter

The Tale of Eleazar was first
published in "Good Housekeeping"
magazine in December 1966.

MY NAME is ELEAZAR.

My life, until the time of which I will tell you, was a quiet one. My master, Joachim, cared for me well. Shelter was mine when needed, poor though it may have been, and there was always enough food to still the pangs of hunger.

My master's dwelling was of stone, patiently hewn out of the rocky hillside, and he himself was a man of great contentment.

He and his wife had but one child, a girl. How can I describe her—who to me is beyond description—bright as the morning star. She used to put her arms round my neck and whisper her secrets to me. Softly breathing, I would nuzzle her gently, pretending that I understood them all, as I longed to do. Though she liked to skip and play with other children, sometimes she would come out alone with me and sit among the anemones which clothed the hills, glowing like fireflies in the early part of the year. When she sat thus, my little mistress seemed to be turning over in her mind the wisdom of the things which her mother and my master, Joachim, taught her so carefully each day. She was clever at weaving and often I would hear her singing while she worked. Tall and lovelier she grew each year and the eyes of men were on her.

Then one day there arrived at my master's door a young man whom I loved at once. His small beard was dark, and his eyes danced as he smiled with his whole face, not just with his lips as some men do. When his glance rested on my little mistress he drew such a breath of wonder that I thought his feet would leave the ground, but there was a wealth of protection in his sigh that made me deeply glad.

He had come to make a stool for my master, for he was a carpenter. He came again with a smooth and polished spindle for my little mistress, and the end was obvious to me even before my long ears were pulled down to hear it.

One morning it was hot, and I was drowsy from the heaviness in the air. Suddenly a fast moving breeze swept across my back. In the distance, for I had strayed in search of grass, I saw our house shimmering as if the wings of a mighty bird were fanning the air around it. A few minutes passed, then all was still, so still that it seemed as if the earth was straining to catch some whispered word. The stillness broke into a sigh and the breeze ruffled my coat again like the hand of an unseen messenger departing. While I stood, my little mistress came out and called to me, and in her voice was such an urgency as if the burden and the joy of all creation were in her. I trotted down quickly to her and the beauty of her face made me tremble.

Then my master brought a saddle bag and placed my lovely woven rug of many colours on my back.

"Take her carefully, Eleazar, he admonished me. Not that I needed to be told. I could pick my way among the rocks as daintily as any turtle dove, which is why I alone was trusted to carry my little mistress. She turned my head up into the hills. How light she was to carry, yet she delighted in walking beside me with just her arm along my neck. So she had been walking when we caught sight of Mistress Zachary coming from her house. Like a stone loosed from David's sling, my little mistress darted forward to meet her—and the greeting exchanged was marvellous to behold.

Whatever news my little mistress had to tell Mistress Zachary took long in sharing, for we stayed many days until

I felt fretful to be home again. My little mistress rode on my back the whole of the homeward way, a thing she had never done before, and I could have sworn that she was heavier.

There was a heaviness in the atmosphere too, and something was amiss at home. Only my little mistress stayed serene. Even her beloved carpenter seemed weighed down by some hidden knowledge, preying heavily on his mind. It hurt me to see his eyes lose their laughter. That night in sleep I sensed again the visit of that mighty bird, and, strangely, when the carpenter came next day, his step was lighter, his face calm, yet full of wonder.

The figs were ripening on the trees, their leaves wide and green, when the wedding feast was made. Oh the weaving and the baking that had first to be done, and the many things which I had to carry hither and thither!

The carpenter's house was full of the perfume of woodshavings from his workshop set in the hillside above the two rooms where he lived. My little mistress loved to watch him working, to see the curling shavings fall from his plane and to feel the sweetness of the hard wood as she ran her fingers along the newly smoothed surface. But I have wandered from the wedding feast.

All the village was gathered there. The fishermen had come up from the lake bringing fine baskets of silver fish. There was newly baked bread, and wine pressed from the choicest grapes; smooth skinned dark green olives and honeycomb from the wild black bees. There was laughter and happiness as the guests washed their hands and feet at the door, and it bubbled everywhere. All jealousy and spite were blown away that day.

My master, Joachim, gave me wholly to my little mistress as a wedding gift, so I followed after her up the hill to the carpenter's house, her new home.

When she became heavy with child I worked harder than I had ever worked before. Every morning and evening they slung the water pitchers across my back. I had to tread deftly from the well so as not to slop the water, and when not a drop was spilt, I was always very well rewarded.

One day, as the hottest time of the year drew near its close, I heard a sound of distant hooves, drumming hard. My ears stood pricked and I cried out with my harsh voice long and loud so that everyone came out to see what was the matter. So they were standing there when, in a cloud of dust, a horseman came riding into the village and pulled so hard on his horse's mouth that it made me wince. The man wore a helmet, and a crimson cloak fell arrogantly from his shoulders over the flanks of his mount. I shrank back as I did not like the whip he carried. As his horse drew to a halt, the Roman soldier waved a scroll of parchment, shouting in a tongue that was strange to me. Leaping down from his horse, he strode towards the synagogue and, taking a dagger from inside his cloak he thrust it through the parchment and hurled it against the wall. All this time not one of the watchers had moved; no one spoke, but I knew from their faces there was hatred for what he had done and for what he was himself.

Then the horseman turned and looked at them. Slowly lifting the helmet from his head and mopping his brow, he made signs that he was thirsty and wanted water. Still no one moved, not even to get him a pitcher to let down the well for himself. He spat on the ground and rounded the horse, jerking the bridle hard. I winced again at the froth round the poor animal's mouth.

He was the one who should have had the cooling drink.

Suddenly my mistress was at his side (the carpenter was away on a day's journey) and in her hands she held a bowl of water. She proffered it to the man and afterwards, oh bless her, she pointed to the horse, who quietened in her presence and drank thankfully.

The man wheeled and, with a last searching look at my mistress, as if to ensure that for all time he would remember her, galloped away.

Then uproar broke out as the villagers ran to see what had been pinned up on the synagogue wall. One of the men held up his hand for quiet while he read out what had been written. The news was received with anger and fretfulness, and I could sense that they felt much as I do sometimes when the flies are hotly buzzing and I want to kick out at anyone near.

Gradually the people dispersed to their own houses and next day there was rain—rain to cool the earth, to wash the pricking dust from my coat and to water down men's tempers.

Whatever was written on that parchment caused such a bringing out of saddlebags such as I had never seen. It must, I guessed, be some order they all had to obey. The whole village seemed to be getting ready to go on a journey—even my mistress, who surely should not go from home at such a time. Nor was it to be a short journey by the look of things.

"Now, Eleazar, be brave for you must bear a heavy burden for a long way", my mistress told me. I lowered my head and rubbed it against her shoulder to tell her that I would carry her all over the world until my heart broke. Even so, I could not help but quail next day when the packs were loaded. For to make room for my mistress to ride, they had to go in front of her and behind across my rump.

The carpenter had fashioned the most beautiful cradle. Hours and hours he had worked on it, while my mistress sat sewing by his side. There were carvings around it of birds and fruit, and, just think, he had even carved me, Eleazar, at the foot. But they could not take the cradle with them, and I wished my back could have been twice as wide, for I saw their sadness at leaving it behind.

We were on our way as soon as the sun's early reflection fingered the whiteness of the dwellings. Everyone moved forward, but as I was the heaviest laden and had to go slowly, we were gradually left behind.

The carpenter walked by my head, always kind and encouraging. It worried my mistress that he should have to walk the whole time, and when we stopped to rest she would bathe his feet after he had seen to mine. Fortunately the air was now cool at this time of year, so we did not have the heat to add to our troubles.

When we reached the best point at which the village could be seen in the far distance, my mistress stopped me and we turned to look back. Had I known then how long a time would pass before we returned, the hazards and the journeyings we would undertake, I think my spirit would have given out then. But as my young Master has since taught me, we have to think only of each present day, and strength is ours for each load as it comes.

We had stopped where two tracks parted. One, boulder strewn, led up into the mountains. The one we were to take stretched away over the grassy plain, following the winding river. The carpenter walked between me and the bank. My mistress spoke rarely, as if to avoid disturbing the rhythm of our pace.

In the evening there was no need to hobble me. They knew I would not stray. I lay near them, listening to their quiet talk until it fluttered into the soft breathing of sleep. At night it seemed to me as if the sky, in its height and depth of darkness, held its breath to watch our progress down the land. Never have I seen such stars. Like candle points they danced and flickered, and the morning star, radiant as my mistress, lingered, suspended in the milky paleness of the dawn, as if reluctant to end its watch over us and give place to the sun's sweeping sword.

Three days and nights we travelled, and, from the increasing shortness of our rest, I sensed the growing urgency that we should reach our journey's end.

On the afternoon of the fourth day we caught sight of a city. The sun clothed the pinnacles of the highest building with a dazzling splendour, making the stones glitter so fiercely that they seemed to twist and blink, hurting my eyes. The carpenter pulled me gently onwards, though I longed to sink down and rest. When his staff struck the paving stones, I heaved a sigh of relief. Now surely we were finished. But this was not so, and we moved on through the narrow streets, up and down and up, until my feet were sore from the unaccustomed hardness of the way. There were many people round us and mules and donkeys too, with noise everywhere, as we left the city by another gate.

I wondered how much further yet. Each step was weariness, but I knew that I must not fail my mistress. No longer could I look ahead. I saw only the ground in front of each successive step.

Suddenly I felt my mistress shudder. Out of the corner of my eye I saw a tall piece of wood with a crosspiece, stuck in the ground. The shadow of it fell across us and in my imagination it added to the weight upon my back.

Soon we were on soft ground once more. If only we had not to hurry so!

We had been joined since leaving the city, by other travellers. Sometimes their mules stopped, refusing to budge further, and I had to stand and wait. The carpenter would leave my head and help the beasts, sometimes quietly changing a pack here and there to ease their burdens. He always managed to get them moving again and his smile, when he returned to my mistress, brightened the darkening night around us.

Once, looking sideways, I glimpsed, in the starlight, flocks of sheep on the hillside, and against the skyline, I saw outlines of the shepherds keeping watch.

I do not know how long we travelled, but it was still night when we came to the next city. There were throngs of people everywhere. This was our journey's end, for the carpenter stopped before an inn. A man came out and pointed down the road, shrugging his shoulders. Again we moved on. Were we to have no rest that night?

At our next halt, no one would answer our knocking. The carpenter knocked then at every dwelling, for if rest and shelter had been urgent for my mistress before, now her need was desperate. Even the carpenter's face grew stern until, at one poor dwelling, a woman thrust past the man who came first to the door and stared at my mistress. Her face softened and she spoke quietly to her. When she turned I saw that she, too, was with child. She beckoned to her husband and they told us to follow them round the side of the house to where I could hear a beast lowing. They brought us bundles of sweet smelling hay and spread them around, then tethering the ox in the corner of his stall, they left us. I sank down on my knees exhausted as soon as the packs were off and must have instantly fallen asleep.

I awoke to the sound of a baby crying.

There in front of me he lay in my mistress' lap, wrapped in all the baby clothes she had been making for so many weeks. How small he looked my little Master. A wisp of hair curled around his forehead and his eyes were tightly shut.

At his feet there knelt a youth like the tallest spike of a lily. There were hushed and wondering voices and people coming in and out.

What followed then has been told time and time again. But no one has ever told of my pride and joy that I, Eleazar,

Mary's donkey, carried on my back the Lord of all creation, before He even came into this world. So did I carry Him too, all through His babyhood, in and out of strange and far-off lands, until the day, when, sitting on my back in front of His mother, with her husband, Joseph the carpenter leading me, my young Master came down the rocky path with His hands around my neck, home at last to Nazareth.

Printed in the United States
By Bookmasters